STOP
PUSHING MY
BUTTONS

LaTusha Sheckles & Thomas Moyler Jr.

DEDICATION

This book is dedicated to all of the innocent victims of cyber bullying or any form of bullying. Lives have been ruined and some even taken because of this senseless immature act…BULLYING

Rest In Heaven

Gabriel Taye
Jackson Grubb
Asad Khan
Morgan Musson

And to all not listed we send our deepest condolences.
A portion of all proceeds will go to causes to prevent bullying.

CHARACTERS

Dale
Intellee
Tabatha
Mr. Appleton
Kindell
Mr. Window
Mom & Dad

Use empty spaces to draw what you think the characters in the book look like. Take a picture, or scan the images and send to:
caremoreproductions@gmail.com
Please include your name and email address and your images may be featured in the follow-up, 2nd installment to the bullying series of,
"STOP PUSHING MY BUTTONS"

CHAPTER 1

Hi, my name is Dale. Today my gigabytes are moving at top speed. All because I will be transferred to a new technology class with all new friends. Yes, I was sad to leave my old class and friends, who were all being sent to a new school all together.

Last year my grades weren't so good. So I was left behind a year. This means I am older, much bigger than the new kids. I hummed with joy as the teacher took me to my new class.

When I entered the class, all the kids looked clean, nice, and happy. I smiled big when the teacher informed the other kids of who I am. The teacher had me sit between two nice kids. On the right of me is a boy named Intellee; on my left is a girl named Tabatha. I couldn't wait to get to know them better.

I would have to wait. Our teacher, Mr. Appleton, began giving us all work to do before he left the class. With Mr. Appleton gone, the class began to whisper, giggle, or point in my direction. I smiled, waving to each of them. Intellee got the whole class's attention with a beautiful picture on his screen. Everyone oohed and aahed. I was very impressed. My screen began to glow with excitement until the kids laughed at my screen. I dimmed with embarrassment.

Intellee made matters worse when he challenged me to make my colors brighter than his. I did not want to look like a loser, so I accepted Intellee's challenge. His screen filled with amazing, beautiful colors: red, green, blue, purple, even colors I'd never seen before. The whole class clapped for Intellee; so did I. Intellee said, "It's your turn, Dale."

With all my might I tried to show on my screen the same colors as Intellee. I did my very best, only to have the kids laugh at me. I wanted this challenge to be over, so I told Intellee, "You win," with a smile.

I went back to doing my assignment. However, Intellee still wished to compete. "Hey, Dale, bet you can't download faster than me."

I didn't want to play any more games. I told Intellee, "No, maybe some other time."

I did not feel that I said anything to upset Intellee, although I must have. Suddenly, Intellee became very mean. "Why? Because you're slow, fat, old, and ugly."

At first I was shocked, then hurt. I only wanted to be Intellee's friend. The other kids pointed, laughing, joining Intellee in taunting me with all kinds of names. Everyone except Tabatha.

Tears ran down my screen. "That's not nice!" I said, only making Intellee talk about me more.

"You're dumb too. You were left behind a year, that's why you can't upload faster than me, either."

My feelings were so hurt. I shouted back, "No, I am not dumb."

Intellee replied, "You're not better than me or the other kids. We are all upgraded. You're just fat with no style."

Tears ran down my screen faster. Mr. Appleton walked back into the class. The kids went back to their work. I thought of telling Mr. Appleton of all the bad things Intellee said to me, but I did not want to be a tattletale. I wiped my tears, did my work.

Tomorrow, I will just sit silently. I won't play Intellee's games at all. That way the kids cannot laugh at me. Soon we'll be friends. I hope tomorrow is a better day.

Well, well, well,

what do we have here?

I'm so new school

and you're so last year.

You're out, I'm in.

You lose, I win.

I'm just so popular

and you have no friends.

CHAPTER 2

Boy, was I glad to be going home. I felt lonely walking to the bus. All the way home I looked out the window, thinking of all the mean things Intellee said. Even when I tried to stop thinking about the unkind words, they would re-enter my brain.

I got home and tossed my book bag in my room before heading to the kitchen for a snack. Mom asked how my day went as I reached the kitchen. I said, "Okay, I guess."

Mom smiled while continuing to prepare dinner. My father appeared in the kitchen from work, kissed my mom, then asked me, "How's it going, pal?"

"Okay," I replied, eating my cookie. "Dad, can I ask you a question?"

My father pulled out a chair across from my own. "Sure, son. What is it?"

I looked to the floor, then to my father. "Dad, why am I so different from the other kids?"

"Son, what do you mean? You're a kid, they're kids. Different how?"

"Well, I'm bigger than the other kids. I can't do everything great like the other kids. I do not think I am as handsome as other boys," I said.

My father chuckled before telling me, "Son, you're a fine kid. You look like me. Also the other kids, some of them cannot do some of the things you can do. God made us all beautiful; we all must be different or else the world would be a pretty boring place. Would you want to live in a place where everyone thought, acted, walked, and talked the same?"

I gave what my father said some thought, thinking, *He is right. I can do things Intellee can't do.* I answered, "No."

Mom joined the conversation. "Son, I am a girl. You and I are different. Does that make me better than you?"

"No," I said.

"Just think, son, how would I know you belonged to me if you looked like everyone else? So you should thank God for making you one of a kind," Mom said.

"Thanks, Mom and Dad."

I finished my cookie and went to my room to play video games.

Mom looked in to ask me, "Son, is everything okay? Why did you ask that question?"

"Nothing, Mom. I was just wondering, but it's fine now. I understand I was meant to be different like everyone else."

"Okay. Dinner will be ready soon."

"Okay, Mom."

The thought of the mean words did not hurt now as much as they did before. Mom and Dad really helped. I will be ready for school tomorrow.

Mom and Dad

It's okay to be different.

Tell the world, say it loud.

Shout I love being me!

Hold your head up and be proud.

Remember Jesus loves you,

this I know,

a perfect creation

from head to toe.

CHAPTER 3

The next day school began great. Mr. Appleton had no reason to leave class unattended, therefore none of the kids poked fun at me. Intellee seemed to be doing his work. At one point he even smiled at me. So I figured all was forgotten.

At lunchtime Mr. Appleton excused the class to eat. We walked in a single file line to the lunch room. Today was my favorite: corn dogs with French fries. After receiving my tray, I took a seat next to Tabatha, who said, "Hi."

I said, "Hi."

While I was eating, I got a bad feeling. When I looked up, most of the kids were laughing and pointing in my direction. My screen started to spin. I noticed Intellee at his table showing the kids his Facebook page: pictures of me crying in class yesterday. Intellee did not stop there. He made YouTube videos and Instagram pictures of me also.

I began to cry. Tabatha grabbed my hand to comfort me. She said, "Don't cry. Pay Intellee no mind. He is just a cyber-bully. You cannot let him know he is getting to you because he will only do it all the time."

I put my hands on my screen to wipe my tears. I asked Tabatha, "What did I ever do to him?"

"You did not have to do anything. That's how bullies are. They don't like themselves, so they put others down to try to forget their own faults or to keep people from seeing their flaws."

Intellee noticed Tabatha speaking to me. So he put her on his social sites too.

The kids started to leave the lunchroom, each of them still giggling at me on their way back to class. Intellee stopped past our table. His Instagram showed a picture of me crying with Tabatha holding my hand. The words read "Sissy" on his screen.

I tried to be strong like Tabatha said, but my feelings were hurt. I could not hold back my tears.

On my way back to class, I stopped in the restroom to clean my screen. I had enough of Intellee. I was going to tell Mr. Appleton about all the mean things Intellee had been doing. My mind made up, I started out of the restroom, only to bump into Intellee. He pushed me back into the restroom.

I said, "Stop. I'm telling Mr. Appleton of all the mean things you have done to me."

Intellee became very angry. He grabbed me by the shirt front. His screen began to glow bright red. He said, "And if you do I'll break your screen, plus I'll tell everyone you're a sissy tattle-tale."

I begged Intellee to let me go. "You're hurting me. Let me go."

Intellee said, "If you tell, I'll really hurt you. Now go back to class, ugly, and keep your big fat mouth closed."

I rushed out of the restroom. The rest of the class began their work by the time I returned.

I was doing my work, hoping to forget Intellee with all his ugly words. Tabatha sent me an E-mail. The E-mail read, "Beware! Intellee plans to beat you up after school."

I became really sick. I asked Mr. Appleton if I could be allowed to go to the nurse. My plan was to get Mom or Dad to come pick me up so I would not have to fight Intellee. Mr. Appleton allowed me to go.

My screen was blue. The nurse called Mom to come get me.

I sent Tabatha an E-mail to say "Thank you." Hopefully Mom will not make me come to school tomorrow. I hope not.

Dale

Bully, bully, bully,

don't be so mean,

In the classroom, hallway,

and computer screen.

You're everywhere I turn,

you're everywhere I look,

on Instagram, Twitter,

even Facebook.

Sticks and stones may break my bones,

but words can hurt as bad.

All the things you write about me

really make me sad.

CHAPTER 4

I did not talk to Mom on the way home from school. My feelings were too hurt. I just felt like the world was against me.

At home, inside my room, I cried, thinking of all the mean things said by the other kids and Intellee. The images from the social sites played over and over in my head, tormenting me. I did nothing to deserve this. I treat people well, I help anyone I can. I like to have fun and laugh, as long as my laughter does not affect anyone else.

Laying with my screen in my pillow, I told myself it would be easier to unplug; if I unplug, it will all be over. No more being different. No more pain. The kids could not be mean to me anymore. Intellee would not be able to beat me up. *Yes, I will unplug. I don't want to live in this ugly world any longer.*

As I got up to unplug, I received a message on Facebook from Tabatha. "How are you feeling, Dale?"

I responded, "Not so great. My feelings are hurt."

"You should not let it get to you. You're a nice person," Tabatha said.

"Tabatha, I try to be nice. I've got no friends. I want to unplug."

"No! Never say that. You have friends. I am your friend."

"Thanks."

"You have to focus on the things you do have. You need to tell your parents about being bullied so they can help."

"But Tabatha, if I do that Intellee will tell the other kids that I am a sissy tattletale."

"Dale, Intellee only told you that because he is afraid of getting into trouble for doing wrong. So who is really the sissy, the person telling or the one afraid of being told on?"

"Well, I guess you got a point. I am not scared of Intellee. I'd rather be nice to people. It takes a lot of energy to be mean. It takes no effort to be nice," I said.

"Well, Intellee must be exhausted," Tabatha said. We both laughed.

I began to feel better. "Thanks for being my friend, Tabatha."

"No problem, Dale, it's easy. You're a handsome kid."

My screen turned light red. Tabatha made me blush.

"You think so?" I said.

"Sure, all the girls in school do."

"Okay, Tabatha, now you are just saying that."

"No, I am not. You don't have to believe me. Anyway, do you want to meet at the playground after you tell your parents about Intellee?"

"Yes, I'll meet you there."

"Dale, you have to promise me one thing."

"What's that, Tabatha?"

"Never, ever think of unplugging again, no matter how big the problem. Friends for life, okay?"

"Okay, Tabatha, I promise. Friends for life."

"See you at the park," she said.

I replied, "See you then."

I got myself together and walked into the living room, where my parents were. I took a seat in my favorite chair. I said, "Mom, Dad, I got something I need to tell you."

Mom and Dad focused on me. Mom said, "What is it, son?"

"Well, today when I went to the nurse, I was not really sick. There's this kid at school named Intellee. He is a bully. He makes fun of me all the time, then he gets the other kids to help him."

My dad asked, "Did you tell the teacher?"

"No, because I didn't want to be a tattletale."

"Son, I'm glad you told us. You can never be a tattletale for doing what's right. How long has this been going on?"

"Since I got in my new class," I said.

I did not realize I was crying. So was my mom, who got up to hug me. "Shh, shh. Don't cry. What did he say about you?" Mom asked.

I showed her all the social sites Intellee talked about me on.

"Son, you did the right thing by coming to us. Next time please tell your teacher, no matter what the other kids say or do, understand?" Dad said.

I shook my head yes.

"We're going to school tomorrow to fix this."

I smiled. "Thanks, Mom and Dad."

My dad smiled. "Give me a hug, champ."

I got up to hug my dad. "Dad, can I go to the playground to see my friend?"

"Sure, have fun."

"I will."

On my way out my parents stopped me. "Son, we love you."

I smiled. "I love you both too," I said, then ran to the play-ground.

Dale

A bully is someone

who has issues with themselves,

so it makes them feel better

to put down someone else.

Remember, life is a gift

and it's yours to enjoy,

so never let anyone's misery

steal your joy.

Always love yourself,

no matter what others may say.

You may be sad right now,

but tomorrow is a new day!

CHAPTER 5

The next day at school, Mom and Dad walked in with me to the principal's office. I noticed Intellee in the hall. He looked visibly shaken. I did not want to get Intellee in trouble, although he had to learn a lesson.

The principal, Mr. Window, had Mr. Appleton come to the office with Intellee. Everyone was seated when Mr. Window asked Intellee, "Intellee, have you been causing problems for Dale?"

At first Intellee shook his head no. Then Mr. Window showed Intellee his Facebook page. Intellee said, "I was just messing around."

"Do you call hurting someone's feelings messing around? How would you like it if someone messed around with you?" Mr. Window said.

"Not very much," Intellee said.

"Well, son, for your actions I am going to have to suspend you for ten days. I will tell your parents. Do you not think you owe Dale an apology?" Mr. Window said.

Intellee looked in my direction. "I am sorry, Dale. I did not mean it. I will take the mean things off the sites."

I smiled. "I accept your apology, Intellee."

My dad asked us, "Do you two think that you could be friends now?"

I said, "Yes."

Intellee surprised me when he said, "Yes." We shook hands.

My parents left. Mr. Appleton took me and Intellee back to class.

Half the day passed. Intellee and the other kids gave me no more problems. In fact, all the kids were being extra nice to me.

We were doing graphs when Mr. Appleton introduced a new student named Kindell. Kindell sat on the other side of Intellee. Mr. Appleton told the class to work quietly while he went to the office. When Mr. Appleton left the class, Kindell put his foot on his desk, looked at Intellee, and laughed.

Intellee asked, "What's so funny?"

"You got no style. Anything you can do, I can do better."

Intellee said, "No, you can't."

Kindell did some fast amazing tricks with his screen. Intellee tried but could not keep up.

Kindell laughed. "You're a wuss."

The rest of the class laughed. Intellee's screen turned blue. He began holding back tears.

Tabatha and I looked at one another. *I will not stand for this.*

Before I knew it, I was out of my seat. I told Kindell, "What are you trying to prove by hurting his feelings? If you want us to like you or think you're better than any of us, that's not the way to do it. You had better learn to be nice because Intellee is a friend of mine, and friends stand up for each other. We are all friends. We would like for you to be our friend too, but no one likes a bully. So you think about that."

All the kids clapped for me.

Kindell said, "Sorry, you're right. No one wants to be a bully. Let's be friends. I apologize, Intellee."

"No problem. Thanks, Dale. You're a real friend," Intellee said.

I smiled and took my seat.

Tabatha said, "Dale, that was so brave of you. I am sorry too."

I asked Tabatha, "For what?"

She said, "For standing by when Intellee bullied you. We should never watch someone get bullied. So I apologize."

"Thanks, Tabatha, but you helped keep me from unplugging."

I stood up once more. I told the whole class, "From this point on, we will not be friends with any bullies whatsoever, and we will never stand by and watch anyone get bullied. So when you have a bully, you simply tell them:

"Stop pushing my buttons."

Tabatha

If you see someone getting bullied,

stand up. Don't stand by.

Don't look the other way

while another person cries.

You see, a bully can only do

what you allow them to do.

So be strong, put your foot down,

and let your courage shine through.

It doesn't matter if you're short, tall,

big or small.

Tell them, if you can't say anything nice,

don't say anything at all!!!

THE END

Made in the USA
Middletown, DE
04 January 2021